SADAKO
and the Thousand Paper Cranes

Eleanor Coerr

US $5.99 / CAN $8.99

ISBN 0-14-240113-7

9 780142 401132

5 0 5 9 9>

EAN

Chizuko's gift

Chizuko was pleased with herself. "I've figured out a way for you to get well," she said proudly. "Watch!" She cut a piece of gold paper into a large square. In a short time she had folded it over and over into a beautiful crane.

Sadako was puzzled. "But how can that paper bird make me well?"

"Don't you remember that old story about the crane?" Chizuko asked. "It's supposed to live for a thousand years. If a sick person folds one thousand paper cranes, the gods will grant her wish and make her healthy again." She handed the crane to Sadako. "Here's your first one."

❧

"[The] story speaks directly to young readers of the tragedy of Sadako's death and, in its simplicity, makes a universal statement for 'peace in the world.' " —*The Horn Book*

"The story is told tenderly but with neither a morbid nor a sentimental tone: it is direct and touching." —*BCCB*

PUFFIN MODERN CLASSICS

Charlie and the Chocolate Factory	Roald Dahl
The Devil's Arithmetic	Jane Yolen
A Long Way from Chicago	Richard Peck
My Side of the Mountain	Jean Craighead George
Roll of Thunder, Hear My Cry	Mildred D. Taylor
Sadako and the Thousand Paper Cranes	Eleanor Coerr
The Summer of the Swans	Betsy Byars
Time Cat	Lloyd Alexander
The Westing Game	Ellen Raskin

SADAKO

and the Thousand Paper Cranes

Eleanor Coerr

paintings by Ronald Himler

PUFFIN BOOKS

For Laura, who remembered Sadako

PUFFIN BOOKS

Published by Penguin Group

Penguin Young Readers Group,

345 Hudson Street, New York, New York 10014, U.S.A.

Penguin Books Ltd, 80 Strand, London WC2R ORL, England

Penguin Books Australia Ltd, 250 Camberwell Road,

Camberwell, Victoria 3124, Australia

Penguin Books Canada Ltd, 10 Alcorn Avenue, Toronto, Ontario, Canada M4V 3B2

Penguin Books (N.Z.) Ltd, 182-190 Wairau Road, Auckland 10, New Zealand

First published in the United States of America by G. P. Putnam's Sons,

a division of the Putnam & Grosset Group, 1977

Published by Puffin Books,

a division of Penguin Putnam Books for Young Readers, 1999

This Puffin Modern Classics edition published by Puffin Books,

a division of Penguin Young Readers Group, 2004

1 3 5 7 9 10 8 6 4 2

THE LIBRARY OF CONGRESS HAS CATALOGED

THE G. P. PUTNAM'S SONS EDITION AS FOLLOWS:

Coerr, Eleanor.

Sadako and the Thousand Paper Cranes.

1. Leukemia in children—Juvenile literature. 2. Sasaki, Sadako, 1943–1955—Juvenile
literature. 3. Atomic bomb—Physiological effect—Juvenile literature.
4. Hiroshima—Bombardment, 1945—Juvenile literature. [1. Leukemia. 2. Sasaki,
Sadako, 1943–1955. 3. Atomic bomb—Physiological effect. 4. Hiroshima—
Bombardment, 1945. 5. Death—Fiction.] I. Himler, Ronald. II. Title.
RJ416.L4C63   362.7'8'19615590   (B)   (92)   76-9872
ISBN 0-399-23799-2

This edition ISBN 0-14-240113-7

Printed in the United States of America

CONTENTS

Prologue   7

1 Good Luck Signs   9

2 Peace Day   15

3 Sadako's Secret   21

4 A Secret No Longer   28

5 The Golden Crane   33

6 Kenji   40

7 Hundreds of Wishes   48

8 Last Days   52

9 Racing With the Wind   60

Epilogue   64

About the Author and This Book   65

How to Fold a Paper Crane   69

PROLOGUE

Sadako and the Thousand Paper Cranes is based on the life of a real little girl who lived in Japan from 1943 to 1955.

She was in Hiroshima when the United States Air Force dropped an atom bomb on that city in an attempt to end World War II. Ten years later she died as a result of radiation from the bomb.

Her courage made Sadako a heroine to children in Japan. This is the story of Sadako.

GOOD LUCK SIGNS

Sadako was born to be a runner. Her mother always said that Sadako had learned to run before she could walk.

One morning in August 1954 Sadako ran outside into the street as soon as she was dressed. The morning sun of Japan touched brown highlights in her dark hair. There was not a speck of cloud in the blue sky. It was a good sign. Sadako was always on the lookout for good luck signs.

Back in the house her sister and two brothers were still sleeping on their bed quilts. She poked her big brother, Masahiro.

"Get up, lazybones!" she said. "It's Peace Day!"

Masahiro groaned and yawned. He wanted to sleep as long as possible, but like most fourteen-year-old boys, he also loved to eat. When he sniffed the good smell of bean soup, Masahiro got up. Soon Mitsue and Eiji were awake, too.

Sadako helped Eiji get dressed. He was six, but he sometimes lost a sock or shirt. Afterward, Sadako folded the bed quilts. Her sister, Mitsue, who was nine, helped put them away in the closet.

Rushing like a whirlwind into the kitchen, Sadako cried, "Oh, Mother! I can hardly wait to go to the carnival. Can we please hurry with breakfast?"

Her mother was busily slicing pickled radishes to serve with the rice and soup. She looked sternly at Sadako. "You are eleven years old and should know better," she scolded. "You must not call it a carnival. Every year on August sixth we remember those who died when the atom bomb was dropped on our city. It is a memorial day."

Mr. Sasaki came in from the back porch. "That's right," he said. "Sadako chan, you must show respect. Your own grandmother was killed that awful day."

"But I do respect Oba chan," Sadako said. "I pray for her spirit every morning. It's just that I'm so happy today."

"As a matter of fact, it's time for our prayers now," her father said.

The Sasaki family gathered around the little altar shelf. Oba chan's picture was there in a gold frame. Sadako looked at the ceiling and wondered if her grandmother's spirit was floating somewhere above the altar.

"Sadako chan!" Mr. Sasaki said sharply.

Sadako quickly bowed her head. She fidgeted and wriggled her bare toes while Mr. Sasaki spoke. He prayed that the spirits of their ancestors were

happy and peaceful. He gave thanks for his barbershop. He gave thanks for his fine children. And he prayed that his family would be protected from the atom bomb disease called leukemia.

Many still died from the disease, even though the atom bomb had been dropped on Hiroshima nine years before. It had filled the air with radiation—a kind of poison—that stayed inside people for a long time.

At breakfast Sadako noisily gulped down her soup and rice. Masahiro began to talk about girls who ate like hungry dragons. But Sadako didn't hear his teasing. Her thoughts were dancing around the Peace Day of last year. She loved the crowds of people, the music, and fireworks. Sadako could still taste the spun cotton candy.

She finished breakfast before anyone else. When she jumped up, Sadako almost knocked the table over. She was tall for her age and her long legs always seemed to get in the way.

"Come on, Mitsue chan," she said. "Let's wash the dishes so that we can go soon."

When the kitchen was clean and tidy, Sadako tied red bows on her braids and stood impatiently by the door.

"Sadako chan," her mother said softly, "we aren't leaving until seven-thirty. You can sit quietly until it is time to go."

Sadako plopped down with a thud onto the *tatami* mat. Nothing ever made her parents hurry. While she sat there a fuzzy spider paced across the room. A spider was a good luck sign. Now Sadako was sure the day would be wonderful. She cupped the insect in her hands and carefully set it free outside.

"That's silly," Masahiro said. "Spiders don't really bring good luck."

"Just wait and see!" Sadako said gaily.

❧2❧

PEACE DAY

When the family started out, the air was already warm and dust hung over the busy streets. Sadako ran ahead to the house of her best friend, Chizuko. The two had been friends since kindergarten. Sadako was sure that they would always be as close as two pine needles on the same twig.

Chizuko waved and walked toward her. Sadako sighed. Sometimes she wished that her friend would move a bit faster. "Don't be such a turtle!" she shouted. "Let's hurry so we won't miss anything."

"Sadako chan, go slowly in this heat," her mother called after her. But it was too late. The girls were already racing up the street.

Mrs. Sasaki frowned. "Sadako is always in such a hurry to be first that she never stops to listen," she said.

Mr. Sasaki laughed and said, "Well, did you ever see her walk when she could run, hop, or jump?" There was pride in his voice because Sadako was such a fast, strong runner.

At the entrance to the Peace Park people filed through the memorial building in silence. On the walls were photographs of the dead and dying in a ruined city. The atom bomb—the Thunderbolt—had turned Hiroshima into a desert.

Sadako didn't want to look at the frightening pictures. She held tight to Chizuko's hand and walked quickly through the building.

"I remember the Thunderbolt," Sadako

whispered to her friend. "There was the flash of a million suns. Then the heat prickled my eyes like needles."

"How can you possibly remember anything?" Chizuko exclaimed. "You were only a baby then."

"Well, I do!" Sadako said stubbornly.

After speeches by Buddhist priests and the mayor, hundreds of white doves were freed from their cages. They circled the twisted, scarred Atomic Dome. Sadako thought the doves looked like spirits of the dead flying into the freedom of the sky.

When the ceremonies were over, Sadako led the others straight to the old lady who sold cotton candy. It tasted even better than last year.

The day passed too quickly, as it always did. The best part, Sadako thought, was looking at all the things to buy and smelling the good food. There were stalls selling everything from bean cakes to chirping crickets. The worst part was seeing people with ugly whitish scars. The atom bomb had burned them so badly that they no longer looked human. If any of the bomb victims

came near Sadako, she turned away quickly.

Excitement grew as the sun went down. When the last dazzling display of fireworks faded from the sky, the crowd carried paper lanterns to the banks of the Ohta River.

Mr. Sasaki carefully lit candles inside of six lanterns—one for each member of the family. The lanterns carried names of relatives who had died because of the Thunderbolt. Sadako had written Oba chan's name on the side of her lantern. When the candles were burning brightly, the lanterns were launched on the Ohta River. They floated out to sea like a swarm of fireflies against the dark water.

That night Sadako lay awake for a long time, remembering everything about the day. Masahiro was wrong, she thought. The spider had brought good luck. Tomorrow she would remind him about that.

❧3❧

SADAKO'S SECRET

It was the beginning of autumn when Sadako rushed home with the good news. She kicked off her shoes and threw open the door with a bang. "I'm home!" she called.

Her mother was fixing supper in the kitchen.

"The most wonderful thing has happened!"

Sadako said breathlessly. "Guess what!"

"Many wonderful things happen to you, Sadako chan. I can't even guess."

"The big race on Field Day!" Sadako said. "I've been chosen from the bamboo class to be on the relay team." She danced around the room, gaily swinging her school bag. "Just think. If we win, I'll be sure to get on the team in junior high school next year." That was what Sadako wanted more than anything else.

At supper Mr. Sasaki made a long speech about family honor and pride. Even Masahiro was impressed. Sadako was too excited to eat. She just sat there, grinning happily.

From then on Sadako thought of only one thing—the relay race. She practiced every day at school and often ran all the way home. When Masahiro timed her with Mr. Sasaki's big watch, Sadako's speed surprised everyone. Maybe, she dreamed, I will be the best runner in the whole school.

At last the big day arrived. A crowd of parents, relatives, and friends gathered at the school to watch the sports events. Sadako was so nervous

she was afraid her legs wouldn't work at all. Members of the other team suddenly looked taller and stronger than her teammates.

When Sadako told her mother how she felt, Mrs. Sasaki said, "Sadako chan, it is natural to be a little bit afraid. But don't worry. When you get out there, you will run as fast as you can."

Then it was time for the relay race.

"Just do your best," Mr. Sasaki said, giving Sadako's hand a squeeze. "We'll be proud of you."

The kind words from her parents made the knot in Sadako's stomach loosen. They love me, no matter what, she thought.

At the signal to start, Sadako forgot everything but the race. When it was her turn, she ran with all the strength she had. Sadako's heart was still thumping painfully against her ribs when the race was over.

It was then that she first felt strange and dizzy. She scarcely heard someone cry, "Your team won!" The bamboo class surrounded Sadako, cheering and shouting. She shook her head a few times and the dizziness went away.

All winter Sadako tried to improve her running speed. To qualify for the racing team in junior high she would have to practice every day. Sometimes after a long run the dizziness returned. Sadako decided not to tell her family about it.

She tried to convince herself that it meant nothing, that the dizziness would go away. But it didn't. It got worse. Frightened, Sadako carried the secret inside of her. She didn't even tell Chizuko, her best friend.

On New Year's Eve Sadako hoped she could magically wish away the dizzy spells. How perfect everything would be if she didn't have this secret! At midnight she was in her cozy bed quilts when the temple bells began to chime. They were ringing out all the evils of the old year so that the new one would have a fine beginning. With each ring Sadako drowsily made her special wish.

The next morning the Sasaki family joined crowds of people as they visited their shrines. Mrs. Sasaki looked beautiful in her best flowered silk kimono.

"As soon as we can afford it, I'll buy a kimono for you," she promised Sadako. "A girl your age should have one."

Sadako thanked her mother politely, but she didn't care about a kimono. She only cared about racing with the team in junior high.

Amidst throngs of happy people Sadako forgot her secret for a while. She let the bright joy of the season wash her worries away. At the end of the day she raced Masahiro home and won easily. Above the door were the good luck symbols Mrs. Sasaki had put there to protect them during the new year.

With a beginning like this, how could anything bad happen?

≋4≋

A SECRET NO LONGER

For several weeks it seemed that the prayers and good luck symbols had done their work well. Sadako felt strong and healthy as she ran longer and faster.

But all that ended one crisp, cold winter day in February. Sadako was running in the school yard. Suddenly everything seemed to whirl around her and she sank to the ground. One of the teachers rushed over to help.

"I . . . I guess I'm just tired," Sadako said in a weak voice. When she tried to stand up, her legs went wobbly and she fell down again. The teacher sent Mitsue home to tell Mr. Sasaki.

He left his barbershop and took Sadako to the Red Cross Hospital. As they entered the building Sadako felt a pang of fear. Part of this hospital was especially for those with the atom bomb sickness.

In a few minutes Sadako was in an examining room where a nurse x-rayed her chest and took some of her blood. Dr. Numata tapped her back and asked a lot of questions. Three other doctors came in to look at Sadako. One of them shook his head and gently stroked her hair.

By now the rest of Sadako's family was at the hospital. Her parents were in the doctor's office. Sadako could hear the murmur of their voices. Once her mother cried, "Leukemia! But that's impossible!" At the sound of that frightening word Sadako put her hands over her ears.

She didn't want to hear anymore. Of course she didn't have leukemia. Why, the atom bomb hadn't even scratched her.

Nurse Yasunaga took Sadako to one of the hospital rooms and gave her a kind of cotton kimono to wear. Sadako had just climbed into bed when her family came in.

Mrs. Sasaki put her arms around Sadako. "You must stay here for a little while," she said, trying to sound cheerful. "But I'll come every evening."

"And we'll visit you after school," Masahiro promised.

Mitsue and Eiji nodded, their eyes wide and scared.

"Do I really have the atom bomb disease?" Sadako asked her father.

There was a troubled look in Mr. Sasaki's eyes, but he only said, "The doctors want to make some tests—that's all." He paused. Then he added, "They might keep you here for a few weeks."

A few weeks! To Sadako it sounded like years. She would miss graduation into junior high school. And even worse, she would not be part

of the racing team. Sadako swallowed hard and tried not to cry.

Mrs. Sasaki fussed over Sadako. She plumped the pillows and smoothed the bedspread.

Mr. Sasaki cleared his throat. "Is . . . is there anything you want?" he asked.

Sadako shook her head. All she really wanted was to go home. But when? A cold lump of fear grew in her stomach. She had heard that many people who went into this hospital never came out.

Later Nurse Yasunaga sent the others away so that Sadako could rest. When she was alone, Sadako buried her face in the pillow and cried for a long time. She had never before felt so lonely and miserable.

❧5❧

THE GOLDEN CRANE

The next morning Sadako woke up slowly. She listened for the familiar sounds of her mother making breakfast, but there were only the new and different sounds of a hospital. Sadako sighed. She had hoped that yesterday was just a bad dream. It was even more real when Nurse Yasunaga came in to give her a shot.

"Getting shots is part of being in the hospital," the plump nurse said briskly. "You'll get used to it."

"I just want the sickness to be over with," Sadako said unhappily, "so I can go home."

That afternoon Chizuko was Sadako's first visitor. She smiled mysteriously as she held something behind her back. "Shut your eyes," she said. While Sadako squinted her eyes tightly shut, Chizuko put some pieces of paper and scissors on the bed. "Now you can look," she said.

"What is it?" Sadako asked, staring at the paper.

Chizuko was pleased with herself. "I've figured out a way for you to get well," she said proudly. "Watch!" She cut a piece of gold paper into a large square. In a short time she had folded it over and over into a beautiful crane.

Sadako was puzzled. "But how can that paper bird make me well?"

"Don't you remember that old story about the crane?" Chizuko asked. "It's supposed to live for a thousand years. If a sick person folds one

thousand paper cranes, the gods will grant her wish and make her healthy again." She handed the crane to Sadako. "Here's your first one."

Sadako's eyes filled with tears. How kind of Chizuko to bring a good luck charm! Especially when her friend didn't really believe in such things. Sadako took the golden crane and made a wish. The funniest little feeling came over her when she touched the bird. It must be a good omen.

"Thank you, Chizuko chan," she whispered. "I'll never never part with it."

When she began to work with the paper, Sadako discovered that folding a crane wasn't as easy as it looked. With Chizuko's help she learned how to do the difficult parts. After making ten birds, Sadako lined them up on the table beside the golden crane. Some were a bit lopsided, but it was a beginning.

"Now I have only nine hundred and ninety to make," Sadako said. With the golden crane nearby she felt safe and lucky. Why, in a few weeks she would be able to finish the thousand. Then she would be strong enough to go home.

That evening Masahiro brought Sadako's homework from school. When he saw the cranes, he said, "There isn't enough room on that small table to show off your birds. I'll hang them from the ceiling for you."

Sadako was smiling all over. "Do you promise to hang every crane I make?" she asked.

Masahiro promised.

"That's fine!" Sadako said, her eyes twinkling with mischief. "Then you'll hang the whole thousand?"

"A thousand!" Her brother groaned. "You're joking!"

Sadako told him the story of the cranes.

Masahiro ran a hand through his straight black hair. "You tricked me!" he said with a grin. "But I'll do it anyhow." He borrowed some thread and tacks from Nurse Yasunaga and hung the first ten cranes. The golden crane stayed in its place of honor on the table.

After supper Mrs. Sasaki brought Mitsue and Eiji to the hospital. Everyone was surprised to see the birds. They reminded Mrs. Sasaki of a famous old poem:

Out of colored paper, cranes
come flying into
our house.

Mitsue and Eiji liked the golden crane best. But Mrs. Sasaki chose the tiniest one made of fancy green paper with pink parasols on it. "This is my choice," she said, "because small ones are the most difficult to make."

After visiting hours it was lonely in the hospital room. So lonely that Sadako folded more cranes to keep up her courage.

Eleven . . . I wish I'd get better.

Twelve . . . I wish I'd get better . . .

KENJI

Everyone saved paper for Sadako's good luck cranes. Chizuko brought colored paper from the bamboo class. Father saved every scrap from the barbershop. Even Nurse Yasunaga gave Sadako the wrappings from packages of medicine. And Masahiro hung every one of the birds, as he had promised. Sometimes he strung many on one thread. The biggest cranes flew alone.

During the next few months there were times when Sadako felt almost well. However, Dr. Numata said it was best for her to stay in the hospital. By now Sadako realized that she had leukemia, but she also knew that some patients recovered from the disease. She never stopped hoping that she would get well, too.

On good days Sadako was busy. She did her homework, wrote letters to friends and pen pals, and amused her visitors with games, riddles, and songs. In the evening she always made paper cranes. Her flock grew to over three hundred. Now the birds were perfectly folded. Her fingers were sure and worked quickly without any mistakes.

Gradually the atom bomb disease took away Sadako's energy. She learned about pain. Sometimes throbbing headaches stopped her from reading and writing. At other times her bones seemed to be on fire. And more dizzy spells sent Sadako into deep blackness. Often she was too weak to do anything but sit by the window and look longingly out at the maple tree in the courtyard. She would stay there for hours, holding the golden crane in her lap.

Sadako was feeling especially tired one day when Nurse Yasunaga wheeled her out onto the porch for some sunshine. There Sadako saw Kenji for the first time. He was nine and small for his age. Sadako stared at his thin face and shining dark eyes.

"Hello!" she said. "I'm Sadako."

Kenji answered in a low, soft voice. Soon the two were talking like old friends. Kenji had been in the hospital for a long time, but he had few visitors. His parents were dead and he had been living with an aunt in a nearby town.

"She's so old that she comes to see me only once a week," Kenji said. "I read most of the time."

Sadako turned away at the sad look on Kenji's face.

"It doesn't really matter," he went on with a weary sigh, "because I'll die soon. I have leukemia from the bomb."

"But you can't have leukemia," Sadako said

quickly. "You weren't even born then."

"That isn't important," Kenji said. "The poison was in my mother's body and I got it from her."

Sadako wanted so much to comfort him, but she didn't know what to say. Then she remembered the cranes. "You can make paper cranes like I do," she said, "so that a miracle can happen."

"I know about the cranes," Kenji replied quietly, "but it's too late. Even the gods can't help me now."

Just then Nurse Yasunaga came out onto the porch. "Kenji," she said sternly, "how do you know such things?"

He gave her a sharp look. "I just know," he said. "And besides, I can read my blood count on the chart. Every day it gets worse."

The nurse was flustered.

"What a talker!" she said. "You are tiring yourself." And she wheeled Kenji inside.

Back in her room Sadako was thoughtful. She tried to imagine what it would be like to be ill and have no family. Kenji was brave, that's all. She made a big crane out of her prettiest paper and sent it across the hall to his room. Perhaps it would bring him luck. Then she folded more birds for her flock.

Three hundred and ninety-eight.

Three hundred and ninety-nine . . .

One day Kenji didn't appear on the porch. Late that night Sadako heard the rumble of a bed being rolled down the hall. Nurse Yasunaga came in to tell her that Kenji had died. Sadako turned to the wall and let the tears come.

After a while she felt the nurse's gentle hand on her shoulder. "Let's sit by the window and talk," Nurse Yasunaga said in a kindly voice.

When Sadako finally stopped sobbing, she looked out at the moonlit sky. "Do you think Kenji is up there on a star island?"

"Wherever he is, I'm sure that he is happy now," the nurse said. "He has shed that tired, sick body and his spirit is free."

Sadako was quiet, listening to the leaves on the maple tree rustle in the wind. Then she said, "I'm going to die next, aren't I?"

"Of course not!" Nurse Yasunaga answered with a firm shake of her head. She spread some

colored paper on Sadako's bed. "Come and let me see you fold another paper crane before you go to sleep. After you finish one thousand birds, you'll live to be an old, old lady."

Sadako tried hard to believe that. She carefully folded cranes and made the same wish.

Four hundred and sixty-three.

Four hundred and sixty-four . . .

❧7❧

HUNDREDS OF WISHES

June came with its long, endless rains. Day after day the sky was gray as rain spattered against the windows. Rain dripped steadily from the leaves of the maple tree. Soon everything in the room smelled musty. Even the sheets felt clammy.

Sadako grew pale and listless. Only her parents and Masahiro were allowed to visit her. The bamboo class sent a *Kokeshi* doll to cheer her up. Sadako liked the wooden doll's wistful smile and the red roses painted on its kimono. The doll stood next to the golden crane on Sadako's bedside table.

Mrs. Sasaki was worried because Sadako didn't eat enough. One evening she brought a surprise wrapped in a *furoshiki* bundle. It contained all of Sadako's favorite foods—an egg roll, chicken and rice, pickled plums, and bean cakes. Sadako propped herself up against the pillows and tried to eat. But it was no use. Her swollen gums hurt so much that she couldn't chew. Finally, Sadako pushed the good things away. Her mother's eyes were bright as if she were going to cry.

"I'm such a turtle!" Sadako burst out. She was angry with herself for making her mother sad. She also knew that the Sasaki family had no extra money for expensive food. Tears stung Sadako's eyes and she quickly brushed them away.

"It's all right," Mrs. Sasaki said soothingly. She cradled Sadako in her arms. "You'll be better

soon. Maybe when the sun comes out again . . ."

Sadako leaned against her mother and listened to her read from a book of poems. When Masahiro came, Sadako was calmer and happier. He told her news from school and ate some of the special dinner.

Before Masahiro left, he said, "Oh, I almost forgot! Eiji sent you a present." He dug into his pocket and pulled out a crumpled piece of silver paper. "Here," he said, giving it to his sister. "Eiji said this is for another crane."

Sadako sniffed the paper. *"Ummm!* It smells like candy," she said. "I hope the gods like chocolate."

The three burst out laughing. It was the first time Sadako had laughed in days. It was a good sign. Perhaps the golden crane's magic was beginning to work. She smoothed out the paper and folded a bird.

Five hundred and forty-one . . .

But she was too tired to make more. Sadako stretched out on the bed and closed her eyes. As Mrs. Sasaki tiptoed out of the room, she whispered a poem she used to say when Sadako was little:

"O flock of heavenly cranes
Cover my child with your wings."

❧8❧

LAST DAYS

Near the end of July it was warm and sunny. Sadako seemed to be getting better. "I'm over halfway to one thousand cranes," she told Masahiro, "so something good is going to happen."

And it did. Her appetite came back and much of the pain went away. Dr. Numata was pleased with her progress and told Sadako she could go home for a visit. That night Sadako was so excited she couldn't sleep. To keep the magic working she made more cranes.

Six hundred and twenty-one.

Six hundred and twenty-two . . .

It was wonderful to be home with the family for *O Bon,* the biggest holiday of the year. *O Bon* was a special celebration for spirits of the dead who returned to visit those they had loved on earth.

Mrs. Sasaki and Mitsue had scrubbed and swept the house until it shone. Fresh flowers brightened the table. Sadako's golden crane and *Kokeshi* doll were there, too. The air was filled with smells of delicious holiday food. Dishes of bean cakes and rice balls had been placed on the altar shelf for ghostly visitors.

That night Sadako watched her mother put a lantern outside so that the spirits could find their way in the dark. She let out a happy sigh. Perhaps, just perhaps, she was home to stay.

For several days a steady stream of friends and relatives come to call on the Sasaki family.

By the end of a week Sadako was pale and tired again. She could only sit quietly and watch the others.

"Sadako certainly has good manners now," Mr. Sasaki said. "Oba chan's spirit must be pleased to see how ladylike her granddaughter has become."

"How can you say that!" Mrs. Sasaki cried. "I would rather have our lively Sadako back." She dabbed at her eyes and hurried into the kitchen.

I'm making everyone sad, Sadako thought. She wished she could suddenly turn into her old self. How happy her mother would be then!

As if he knew what was in Sadako's mind, her father said gruffly, "There now, don't worry. After a good night's rest you'll feel fine."

But the next day Sadako had to return to the hospital. For the first time she was glad to be in the quiet hospital room. Her parents sat beside the bed for a long time. Every now and then Sadako drifted off into a strange kind of half-sleep.

"When I die," she said dreamily, "will you put my favorite bean cakes on the altar for my spirit?"

Mrs. Sasaki could not speak. She took her daughter's hand and held it tightly.

"Hush!" Mr. Sasaki said in a funny voice. "That will not happen for many, many years. Don't give up now, Sadako chan. You have to make only a few hundred more cranes."

Nurse Yasunaga gave Sadako medicine that helped her rest. Before her eyes closed, Sadako reached out to touch the golden crane.

"I *will* get better," she murmured to the *Kokeshi* doll, "and someday I'll race like the wind."

From then on Dr. Numata gave Sadako blood transfusions or shots almost every day. "I know it hurts," he said, "but we must keep on trying."

Sadako nodded. She never complained about the shots and almost constant pain. A bigger pain was growing deep inside of her. It was the fear of dying. She had to fight it as well as the disease. The golden crane helped. It reminded Sadako that there was always hope.

Mrs. Sasaki spent more and more time at

the hospital. Every afternoon Sadako listened for the familiar *slap-slap* of her plastic slippers in the hall. All visitors had to put on yellow slippers at the door, but Mrs. Sasaki's made a special sound. Sadako's heart ached to see her mother's face so lined with worry.

The leaves on the maple tree were turning rust and gold when the family came for one last visit. Eiji handed Sadako a big box wrapped in gold paper and tied with a red ribbon. Slowly Sadako opened it. Inside was something her mother had always wanted for her—a silk kimono with cherry blossoms on it. Sadako felt hot tears blur her eyes.

"Why did you do it?" she asked, touching the soft cloth. "I'll never be able to wear it and silk costs so much money."

"Sadako chan," her father said gently, "your mother stayed up late last night to finish sewing it. Try it on for her."

With a great effort Sadako lifted herself out of bed. Mrs. Sasaki helped her put on the kimono and tie the sash. Sadako was glad her swollen legs didn't show. Unsteadily she limped across the

room and sat in her chair by the window. Everyone agreed that she was like a princess in the kimono.

At that moment Chizuko came in. Dr. Numata had given her permission to visit for a short time. She stared at Sadako in surprise. "You look better in that outfit than in school clothes," she said.

Everyone laughed. Even Sadako. "Then I'll wear it to classes every day when I'm well again," she joked.

Mitsue and Eiji giggled at the idea.

For a little while it was almost like the good times they used to have at home. They played word games and sang Sadako's favorite songs. Meanwhile, she sat stiffly in the chair, trying not to show the pain it caused her. But it was worth the pain. When her parents left, they looked almost cheerful.

Before she went to sleep, Sadako managed to fold only one paper crane.

Six hundred and forty-four . . .

It was the last one she ever made.

❧ 9 ❧

RACING WITH THE WIND

As Sadako grew weaker, she thought more about death. Would she live on a heavenly mountain? Did it hurt to die? Or was it like falling asleep?

If only I could forget about it, Sadako thought. But it was like trying to stop the rain from falling. As soon as she concentrated on something else, death crept back into her mind.

Toward the middle of October, Sadako lost track of days and nights. Once, when she was awake, she saw her mother crying.

"Don't cry," she begged. "Please don't cry." Sadako wanted to say more, but her mouth and tongue wouldn't move. A tear slid down her cheek. She had brought her mother so much grief. And all Sadako could do now was make paper cranes and hope for a miracle.

She fumbled with a piece of paper. Her fingers were too clumsy to fold it.

I can't even make a crane, she said to herself. I've turned into a real turtle! Quickly, quickly, Sadako tried with all her strength to fold the paper before she was swept into darkness.

It might have been minutes or hours later that Dr. Numata came in and felt Sadako's forehead. He gently took the paper out of her hands. She barely heard him say, "It's time to rest. You can make more birds tomorrow."

Sadako gave a faint nod. Tomorrow . . . tomorrow seemed such a long, long way off.

The next time she awoke, the family was

there. Sadako smiled at them. She was part of that warm, loving circle where she would always be. Nothing could ever change that.

Already lights were dancing behind her eyes. Sadako slid a thin, trembling hand over to touch the golden crane. Life was slipping away from her, but the crane made Sadako feel stronger inside.

She looked at her flock hanging from the ceiling. As she watched, a light autumn breeze made the birds rustle and sway. They seemed to be alive and flying out through the open window. How beautiful and free they were! Sadako sighed and closed her eyes.

She never woke up.

EPILOGUE:

SADAKO SASAKI died on October 25, 1955.

Her classmates folded 356 cranes so that 1,000 were buried with Sadako. In a way she got her wish. She will live on in the hearts of people for a long time.

After the funeral the bamboo class collected Sadako's letters and her journal and published them in a book. They called it *Kokeshi*, after the doll they had given to Sadako while she was in the hospital. The book was sent around Japan and soon everyone knew about Sadako and her thousand paper cranes.

Sadako's friends began to dream of building a monument to her and all children who were killed by the atom bomb. Young people throughout the country helped collect money for the project. Finally their dream came true. In 1958 the statue was unveiled in the Hiroshima Peace Park. There is Sadako, standing on top of a granite mountain of paradise. She is holding a golden crane in outstretched hands.

A Folded Crane Club was organized in her honor. Members still place thousands of paper cranes beneath Sadako's statue on August 6—Peace Day. They make a wish, too. Their wish is engraved on the base of the statue:

> *This is our cry,*
> *this is our prayer;*
> *peace in the world.*

MORE ABOUT THE AUTHOR AND THIS BOOK:
ELEANOR COERR was born in Kamsack, Saskatchewan, Canada, and grew up in Saskatoon. Two of her favorite childhood hobbies were reading and making up stories.

Her fascination with Japan began when she received a book called *Little Pictures of Japan* one Christmas. It showed children in beautiful kimonos playing games, chasing butterflies, and catching crickets. She pored over the colored illustrations, dreaming of one day joining those children in Japan. Her best friend in high school was a Japanese girl whose family introduced her to brush painting, eating with chopsticks, and origami. Eleanor's desire to visit that magical place never faded, and her well-thumbed copy of that favorite book is still in her library.

Eleanor began her professional life as a newspaper reporter and editor of a column for children. Luckily, she traveled to Japan in 1949 as a writer for the *Ottawa Journal*, since none of the other staff wanted to go to a country that had been devastated by war. To learn Japanese, Eleanor lived on a farm near Yonago for about one year, absorbing the culture and enjoying rural celebrations. Soon she was able to visit nearby schools and speak to young audiences about her country. Eleanor wrote and illustrated *Circus Day* in Japan, using the farm family and a visit to the circus as models. It was published in Tokyo in 1953.

Her most difficult trip while she was in Japan was to Hiroshima. Eleanor was shocked by the horrible destruction and death caused by one atom bomb. Of course, she did not know Sadako Sasaki at that time, although she was living there with her family. The misery and suffering Eleanor witnessed was burned into her mind, and she hoped future world leaders would avoid wars at all costs.

One beautiful day in 1963, Eleanor revisited Hiroshima and saw the statue of Sadako in the Hiroshima Peace Park. Impressed by the stories she heard about Sadako's talent for running, courage when faced with cancer, and determination to fold one thousand paper cranes, Eleanor was inspired to find a copy of *Kokeshi*, Sadako's autobiography.

Eleanor looked everywhere she could think of and asked all of her Japanese friends to help. Since the school had copied the ninety-four pages and stapled them together, most of the books had fallen apart. Years passed, and Eleanor continued writing for newspapers in various countries and wrote more children's books. But she was always hoping to find *Kokeshi*.

One fateful afternoon, Eleanor was having tea with

a missionary who had lived in Hiroshima all through the war.

"Eleanor," she said, "you should write a biography of Sadako Sasaki for American children to read."

"I would love to," said Eleanor, "but I must have *Kokeshi* to get all the true facts about Sadako."

The missionary took Eleanor to her attic. Lo and behold, at the bottom of an old trunk was an original copy of *Kokeshi*. Eleanor rushed to have it translated properly and began writing *Sadako and the Thousand Paper Cranes* as soon as she could.

"It's like magic. I was meant to write her story," Eleanor said.

Sadako and the Thousand Paper Cranes has been translated into many languages and has moved both children and adults to write plays, perform ballets, compose songs, and collect money for peace statues—all celebrating Sadako and her wish for peace. Eleanor has visited schools all around the world, encouraging her audiences to work for a nonviolent world. Folded cranes are everywhere, and always underneath the statue of Sadako in Hiroshima's Peace Park.

Eleanor receives many letters about the effect Sadako's story has had on readers. A few are included on the next page.

Dear Author,

I learned that we dropped a bomb and people died. We also suffered in Pearl Harbor when the Japanese dropped a bomb there. I think Sadako is important because she did not want any more wars to hurt people.

Dear Eleanor Coerr,

My mother is dying of cancer. Her name is Mabel. Please know that she is bravely struggling to live, never complains, and is learning how to fold paper cranes like Sadako. Thank you for writing the Sadako book. It is helping my mother.

Dear Author,

I like your story about Sadako because even though she was sick, she never lost hope. She was steadfast. When I grow up I want to be a writer like you. I am going to make people stop fighting.

Dear Mrs. Coerr,

We are studying about survival in our class. The teacher read your story about Sadako. It taught us to always believe in yourself. And never give up. I will never forget this book. You made the sentences come alive.

HOW TO FOLD A PAPER CRANE
BY GAY MERRILL GROSS

The paper crane that Sadako folded is an example of origami, which in Japanese means folded paper.

Because it symbolizes long life, good health, and good fortune, the origami crane has long been the most popular origami figure in Japan. As the story of Sadako has spread, the paper crane has also come to be known around the world as a symbol of peace.

Beginning on the next page are instructions for you to fold the same origami crane that Sadako made.

For more information on origami and origami books and paper, contact:

OrigamiUSA
15 West 77th Street
New York, NY 10024-5192

(212) 769-5635

www.origami-usa.org

Getting Started:

You will need a square of lightweight paper, approximately 6 to 8 inches square. Special origami paper is available at many toy and craft stores. If your paper is colored on one side only, begin with the colored side facing up.

1.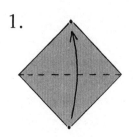

Hint 1: Always do origami on a hard, flat surface.

Fold in half, corner to corner, to make . . .

2.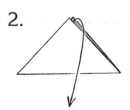

. . . a triangle. Crease sharply and unfold back to a square.

3.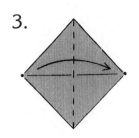

Hint 2: Fold neatly and carefully.

Fold in half again, side corner to side corner.

4.

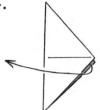

Hint 3: *Make very sharp creases.*

Crease sharply and unfold back to a square.

5.

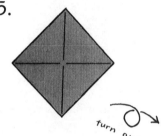

Turn your paper over to the white side and position it as shown in drawing 6.

turn over

Fold in half edge to edge to make . . .

6.

7.

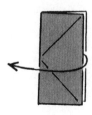

. . . a rectangle. Crease sharply and unfold back to a square.

Fold in half, top edge to bottom edge. This time leave the fold in place.

8.

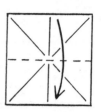

9.

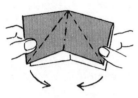

Hold the sides in each hand (as shown) and push your hands down and together.

10.

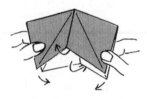

Notice that as you push, the middle of the front and back layers are spreading away from each other. Continue to push your hands down and together until . . .

11.

. . . your paper has collapsed (like an umbrella) and you see four triangular flaps. Pair together two flaps on the right and two flaps on the left.

Flatten your paper and sharpen all folded edges. This multilayered square form is called a Preliminary Base. It is the beginning form for hundreds of origami figures.

12.

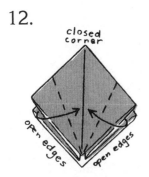

Fold the right and left open edges *(front flaps only)* to the center crease line. Crease sharply.

Checkpoint: *Make sure the pointed bottom of the cone shape you have formed is at the open end of the Preliminary Base.*

13.

You should now see an ice cream cone on top of a diamond-shaped background. Fold the top triangle (the "ice cream") down over the "cone." Crease very sharply.

14.

Unfold the two flaps that form the "cone," but leave the top "ice cream" triangle folded down.

Hint 4: Always look ahead to the next drawing to see the result of the step you are doing.

15.

Lift the very first layer at the bottom corner while holding the other layers in place. As you raise the first layer upward, the "ice cream" triangle should also rise upward until you see . . .

16.

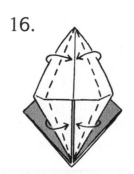

. . . a large mouth form. Fold the long side edges inward along existing creases to meet neatly in the middle.

17.

This forms a tall diamond shape. Smooth your paper flat and neaten the top and bottom corners so they form sharp points. Turn your paper over.

turn over

Repeat steps 12 through 17 on this side.

18.

19.

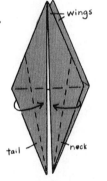

wings

tail   neck

This tall diamond-shaped form is called a Bird Base. The two top flaps will form the crane's wings. At the bottom is a split giving you two thin flaps that will become the neck and tail of the crane.

Narrow the neck and tail by folding the slanted outside edge of each *(front layer only)* to *almost* touch the center split.

Checkpoint: *Make sure you have narrowed the split end (the neck and tail) and not the wing end.*

20.

Here is the result. Turn your paper over and repeat step 19 on the back.

21.

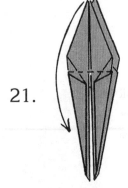

Fold the front wing down *as far as it will go*. Turn your paper over and repeat on the back.

22.

Lift the right half of the *front* wing and swing it to the left as if turning the page of a book. This will cause the slender neck that is sandwiched between the wings to spread open.

23.

Fold up the neck (the long, thin front flap) as high as it will go.

neck

Fold the tip of the neck down as shown to form a head. Crease firmly.

24.

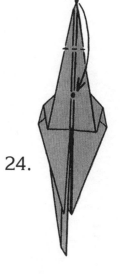

Head

Neck

25. Lift the leftmost *front* flap and swing it to the right. You will again see the wing. The neck and head should be folded neatly in half.

Slide the head out and **26.**
up to the position shown
in drawing 27. Set the
head in place by pinch-
ing the top of the head.

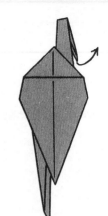

27. Lift the left half of the
front wing and swing it
to the right. This will
cause the slender tail that
is sandwiched between
the wings to spread open.

28.

Fold up the tail (the
long, thin front flap) as
high as it will go.

tail

29.

Lift the rightmost *front* flap and swing it to the left. You will again see the wing. The tail should be folded neatly in half.

Hold the crane at the top of the wings. With your other hand, slide the neck out to the side (see position in next drawing). Set it in place by pressing firmly at the bottom of the neck (which lies hidden between the wings). Repeat on the left, pulling out the tail.

30.

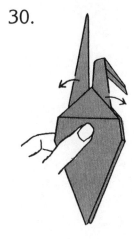

Gently lift the front and back wings and let them rest out at the sides at a slight upward angle.

31.

32.

You may leave the crane's body flat or expand it. To expand, hold a wing in each hand, close to the body, and gently spread your hands apart. Try to give the body a rounded shape.

Your paper crane is finished! If you wish, hang it from a thread. Give it as a token of friendship, good wishes, and peace.

33.

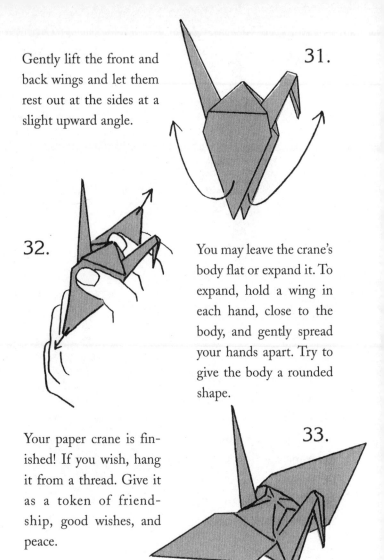